The Mystery of the Weird Beards

'The Mystery of the Weird Beards'
An original concept by Katie Dale
© Katie Dale 2021

Illustrated by Marina Pérez Luque

Published by MAVERICK ARTS PUBLISHING LTD

Studio 11, City Business Centre, 6 Brighton Road,

Horsham, West Sussex, RH13 5BB

© Maverick Arts Publishing Limited November 2021

+44 (0)1403 256941

A CIP catalogue record for this book is available at the British Library.

ISBN 978-1-84886-847-2

Maverick
publishing
www.maverickbooks.co.uk

Grey

This book is rated as: Grey Band (Guided Reading)

The Mystery of the Weird Beards

Written by
Katie Dale

Illustrated by
Marina Pérez Luque

Chapter 1

Danny and Loz gasped as they entered the enormous exhibition hall.

"Wow!" Loz cried. "I've never seen so many inventions!"

Danny's eyes gleamed with excitement. "I wonder what they all do?"

"None of them will be as good as Mum's incredible beard serum," Dad said, smiling as he helped unload Mum's bottle and jars onto her stand. "I can't wait to demonstrate to everyone how it lets me control the length of my beard! It's amazing!"

"Thanks," Mum said, smiling nervously. "But all these inventions look amazing. It's going to be a tough competition."

"Nonsense!" Dad scoffed, looking around. "Who needs a... a self-stirring saucepan or a... a giggle machine?"

"Not you, Dad!" Danny laughed, tickling him. "I can make you giggle anytime, you're so ticklish!"

"Hahaha!" Dad laughed, squirming and giggling and knocking Mum's table, sending the stack of jars and bottles tumbling to the floor.

"Oops!" Danny and Dad said simultaneously as Mum sighed and Loz rolled her eyes. Danny was always getting into trouble!

"Come on, Danny," Loz said, quickly picking up the dropped bottles and jars. "Let's go and look around, and let Mum and Dad set up in peace."

Mum smiled at her gratefully. Danny and Loz wandered around the hall, their eyes wide in wonder.

"Look! There's the Prime Minister!" Danny cried, pointing. "How exciting!"

"He's the guest judge," Loz replied. "He'll present the trophy to the winning inventor—I hope it's Mum!"

"Of course Mum will win," Danny said confidently. "Her invention is amazing—and the Prime Minister has a beard! He'll love it!"

"I hope so," Loz replied. Mum had been working hard for weeks, perfecting her special beard serum. "There are lots of amazing inventions here though. Look—there's a DNA tracker. I wonder how it works…"

"I'll show you, if you like?" the scientist behind the stand said, smiling.

"That would be wonderful!" Loz smiled, pulling out her mobile phone. "Could I record a video interview for our school paper?"

"Of course!" the scientist agreed.

Danny rolled his eyes. There were *way* more interesting inventions than a DNA tracker! His eyes fell on a stand labelled 'Never-ending toffee!'. Danny licked his lips. Now *that* was more like it! Toffees were his favourite! But could a toffee *really* last *forever*…? There was only one way to find out!

"So, how does your invention work?" Loz asked the DNA scientist, filming him on her phone.

"Well, it's really very easy," he explained. "You simply put something that has DNA in it—a hair for example—into this tube, and then the screen will show you where that person is."

"Amazing!" Loz beamed. "And how did you—"

"Loz!" Danny ran up suddenly and grabbed her arm. "Run!"

"What?!" Loz looked round to see an angry man running towards Danny. "What've you done *now?*"

"I ate his toffee!" Danny cried as they ran. "I didn't know it was the only one! Quick—*hide!*"

Chapter 2

Danny and Loz hid behind a curtain just as the angry toffee scientist ran past. Phew!

"Why are you always getting into trouble, Danny?" Loz hissed.

"I didn't know it was his only toffee!" Danny protested. "I wanted to see if it really was never-ending, but I guess now we'll never know—when he started chasing me, I swallowed it!"

"Seriously? A never-ending toffee?" Loz rolled her eyes. "You'd have been better off trying that green potion there—it says it'll increase your brain power! Maybe then you'd think before you act!"

Danny peered at the green potion and the female scientist stirring it. He pulled a face. "It doesn't look as tasty as the toffee..."

Suddenly the female scientist's mobile phone rang. She hastily brushed her hair, put on a silver headband, then answered the phone.

"Hello!" she beamed at the screen. "Do we have a deal?"

"No," came a voice from the phone. "A million pounds is far too expensive. We'll offer five hundred thousand— *if* your invention wins the contest."

The scientist's bright smile disappeared into a frown, and she lowered her voice.

"It doesn't need to *win*," she hissed. "That's the beauty of my plan! I just need the Prime Minister to have the tiniest sip."

Danny and Loz stared at each other. What was she talking about?

"But how will you get the Prime Minister to drink it?" the voice on the phone asked.

The scientist rolled her eyes. "Because, you fool, everyone *thinks* it's a potion to increase brain power— they don't know it's a mind control potion!"

Danny's eyes widened and Loz gasped. Then the scientist turned—and saw them!

"Quick!" Loz cried. "Run!"

Danny and Loz darted and dashed through the exhibition hall, the female scientist hot on their heels.

"Come back here, you naughty kids!" she cried.

"This way, Loz!" Danny called, jumping over a robotic dog.

"Woof woof!" the dog barked suddenly, startling Loz. She shrieked and stumbled into a large box.

"Hey!" a man yelled as the box spilled marbles all over the floor.

"I'm so sorry!" Loz called over her shoulder.

"Argh!" the female scientist shrieked, slipping and sliding on the marbles. "Stop those kids!"

A burly security guard hurried over.

"Look out, Danny!" Loz called as a guard blocked their path.

"Stop!" ordered a security guard—but Danny ducked and slid straight through his legs.

"I'm so *not* sorry!" Danny grinned, sprinting away.

"Oi! Come back here!" the security guard yelled.

"What's going on?" Mum and Dad looked up as Danny and Loz rushed back to her stand, followed by the security guard and the female scientist.

"She's an evil scientist!" Danny panted, pointing at the woman.

"She's going to use a mind control potion to control the Prime Minister!" Loz puffed.

"What?!" Mum gasped. "Are you sure?"

"What nonsense!" the female scientist laughed. "What imaginative children you have!"

Dad frowned. "They may be imaginative, but they don't lie." He turned to the security guard. "This woman should be arrested."

The security guard looked from Danny and Loz to the female scientist, looking uncertain.

"You can't arrest me!" she scoffed. "I'm Marissa Hendricks, award-winning scientist! Besides, you have no proof! These children are just making up stories to help their mother win the contest!"

The security guard raised an eyebrow. "Do you have any proof, kids?"

Danny sighed. Grown-ups never believed kids without proof. It was so unfair. Grown-ups lied *way* more than kids!

"Um… Yes, actually, we *do* have proof!" Loz cried suddenly, looking at her phone. "My video was still recording after my interview with the DNA guy!" She rewound the recording and showed the security guard the video of Marissa on the phone.

Danny grinned. Loz was so smart. Often it was really annoying, but occasionally—like now—it came in handy!

"Everyone *thinks* it's a potion to increase brain power!" Marissa's recorded voice hissed. "They don't know it's a mind control potion!"

"See!" Danny cried. "We're telling the truth! She was going to use it on the Prime Minister!"

Marissa's face turned white, then purple, her mouth opening and closing like a goldfish.

The security guard grabbed her arm. "You're coming with me!"

"Yes!" Danny punched the air. "We did it!"

"Thank goodness!" Loz sighed with relief.

"Imagine if she'd got away with it!" Mum gasped.

"Well done, you two!" Dad beamed, hugging them all.

Chapter 3

Finally, it was time for all the inventions to be judged. Mum bit her lip nervously as the judges approached her stand.

"What does your invention do?" the Prime Minister asked her, smiling.

"It um... um..." Mum stuttered nervously. "Um..."

"Watch and see!" Dad interjected, pasting some of the yellow serum on his chin. Immediately hair began to grow and, within moments, Dad had a thick beard.

"Wow!" the Prime Minister gasped. "That's amazing!"

"The best part is that you can control exactly how long you want the beard to grow," Dad said. "The more serum you use, the longer the beard."

"Incredible!" the Prime Minister beamed. "Can I try it? I can never get my beard to grow more than a centimetre or so!"

"Of course!" Mum beamed at him. "Help yourself!"

Loz and Danny grinned at each other. This was going so well!

The Prime Minister pasted his chin with Mum's yellow serum, and immediately a large beard began to grow.

"This is great!" he cried. "But… what's wrong with your husband?"

Dad's eyes had glazed over and he looked weird. "What do you command?" he said in a strange voice.

"Dad?" Loz said. "Are you okay?"

"He's just messing around," Mum laughed nervously. "He's always joking!"

But suddenly the Prime Minister started to look strange too. "What do you command?" he asked.

"What?" Mum replied, flustered. "What's going on? Is this a joke?"

"What do you command?" Dad and the Prime Minister repeated.

"Sir, are you okay?" the security guard asked, waving his hand in front of the Prime Minister's face. He didn't even blink. "What's wrong with him?"

"It's the weird beards!" one of the other judges cried. "The serum's affected their brains!"

"What? No! That's impossible!" Mum cried.

"What do you command?" Dad and the Prime Minister repeated together.

Loz and Danny looked at each other nervously.

"Whatever you did, undo it!" the security guard demanded.

"But I didn't do anything!" poor Mum protested, looking very pale. "This has never happened before!"

Suddenly Loz spotted a small pool of green liquid spilled on the table next to the pots of yellow serum. "It must have been Marissa!" Loz cried, pointing at it. "She must have mixed some of her mind control potion in with Mum's serum!"

"Of course!" Danny gasped. "That makes sense!"

"That's impossible," the security guard said, frowning. "I escorted Marissa from the building ages ago. She can't get back in—plus you'd have seen her near your stand."

"I've been here the whole time," Mum agreed, frowning. "I haven't seen her. The only people who've been near my stand are my family, the judges, and the security guard."

"Speaking of which, what were you two doing near Marissa's stand in the first place?" the security guard asked Danny and Loz. "Stealing her mind control potion?"

"What? No!" Loz gasped. "Of course not!"

"I think you did," the security guard continued, his frown deepening. "I think you stole some of her mind control potion and mixed it with your mum's serum, then reported Marissa to get rid of the competition!"

"No!" Danny protested. "We didn't! We're not that clever! At least, *I'm* not…"

Loz rolled her eyes.

"Either way, you're all coming with me until we get to the bottom of this—and the Prime Minister is back to normal! I'm calling the police!" The security guard grabbed Mum's arm, but Danny and Loz were too quick and darted away before he could grab them.

"We have to prove Mum's innocent!" Loz cried as they sprinted away.

"And get Dad and the Prime Minister back to normal!" Danny added. "And not get caught ourselves!"

Chapter 4

"I don't understand!" Loz whispered, as they hid in a broom cupboard. "How could Marissa's potion have got into Mum's serum if she's locked out of the building?"

"Unless she isn't," Danny said. "What if she snuck back in somehow?"

"I guess there's only one way to find out," Loz said.

Danny frowned. "How?"

Loz's eyes twinkled. "The DNA locator! We could use it to find out where she is!"

"You want to *steal* an invention?" Danny gasped. "Who are you, and what have you done with my sensible sister!

Loz rolled her eyes. "Some things are more important than following all the rules. Like saving Mum, Dad, and the Prime Minister! Besides, it's not stealing—it's borrowing!"

Together, they crept carefully through the exhibition hall, ducking under tables and hiding behind inventions whenever security guards walked past. Finally, they made it to the DNA tracker scientist's stand.

"Back again?" he smiled at Loz.

"Um yes," Loz smiled nervously, trying to distract him as Danny snuck behind the stand. "I-I didn't get to finish my interview earlier, and... and I have a few more questions—if that's okay?"

She crossed her fingers and bit her lip. She hated fibbing... but it was for a good cause...

Danny flashed her a thumbs-up as he grabbed the machine and ducked under a table.

"Sure," the scientist replied. "Fire away!"

"Oh!" Loz said, flustered. "Oh... silly me, I've forgotten my phone, I'll just go and get it!" She hurried away and joined Danny beneath the table.

"Nice one!" Danny grinned. "Now what?"

"Now we need some of Marissa's DNA..." Loz said. "I know! Her hairbrush! She left it on her stand when her phone rang!"

"Let's hope it's still there!" Danny said, crossing his fingers.

They were in luck! While Loz kept watch, Danny crawled beneath Marissa's table, grabbed her brush, and pulled a handful of hair off it. "Eww! Gross!" he cringed, handing it to Loz.

She put the hair in the DNA tracker and held her breath. "That should be all we need, but why isn't the machine doing anything?"

"Have you turned it on?" Danny suggested, pressing a red button. The screen immediately lit up. Danny grinned. "I thought you were supposed to be the smart one?"

Loz rolled her eyes. "I am—that's why I don't just press random buttons! Anything could've happened!"

Danny shrugged. "It worked, didn't it?"

Sure enough, a green dot appeared on the screen.

"She's close by!" Loz gasped. "She's in the building!"

"Then what are we waiting for?" Danny asked. "Let's find her!"

Chapter 5

They followed the green dot through the building, along a long corridor, and towards a back room. Suddenly they heard Marissa's voice, and froze.

"Find those children!" she hissed behind a half-open door.

"Who's she talking to?" Danny frowned. "There's no one else in the room, and she's not on the phone."

"The mind control potion must work remotely!" Loz gasped. "Whoever's taken the potion can hear her orders wherever they are—that's so dangerous!"

"What do you mean the kids have disappeared?" Marissa snapped. "They have to be here somewhere!

If they tell the police that I added my mind control potion to their mum's beard serum, they'll ruin everything! They're all that stand between me and my master plan!"

"She's right!" Danny grinned, lunging forward. "And we're going to stop her!"

"No—wait!" Loz hissed, grabbing his arm. "We need evidence that she's the person behind the mind control first! And we need to work out *how* she's controlling everyone!"

She pulled out her mobile phone and pressed record, edging closer.

"Now, Prime Minister," Marissa continued. "Call the Treasury, and tell them to transfer ten million pounds into the following account…"

"*Ten million!*" Danny hissed, "Imagine how many toffees you could buy with that!" He whirled round to face Loz—and knocked her arm! Loz's mobile slipped from her fingers and tumbled to the floor with a loud clatter!

"Oops!" Danny winced as Loz turned deathly pale.

Suddenly the door flew wide open and Marissa scowled at them. "Guard, get here at once and grab these children!" she ordered.

"Loz! Run!" Danny cried.

"Not without my phone!" Loz said, grabbing for it, but Marissa kicked it, sending it skittering across the floor.

"Leave it, Loz!" Danny yelled, grabbing her hand.

"I can't!" Loz insisted, pulling away and running after it. "We need it to help Mum and Dad!"

"But we can't help them if we get caught!" Danny argued. "Come on!"

But it was too late. As Loz picked up her phone, heavy footsteps ran down the corridor: it was Dad, the Prime Minister—and the security guard!

"The security guard's being controlled too!" Loz gasped as the Prime Minister pinned her arms behind her back. "Of course! She must have given him her mind control potion when he evicted her from the building—and *he* must have put her potion in Mum's serum!"

"Clever girl," Marissa smiled. "But you're too late."

"Dad! Stop!" Danny cried as his father grabbed him. "It's me! Danny! Let me go!"

But it was no good. His dad's grip was like a vice.

"Bring them in here!" Marissa ordered, and the men obeyed. She locked the door and smiled smugly.

"Dad, let me go! Snap out of it! Danny begged, but Dad's eyes were still glazed over, his grip tight. "Dad please! Loz is in danger!"

"She isn't in danger," Marissa said, reaching for something in her pocket. "Neither of you are, as long as you do what you're told!"

"Fat chance!" Danny scoffed. "I *never* do what I'm told!"

"You'll never get away with this!" Loz yelled as Marissa walked towards her. "I have evidence of your evil plot. You're going to jail for a looong—"

Quick as a flash, Marissa poured a droplet of green liquid into Loz's open mouth. Loz's eyes widened in horror.

"NO!" Danny wailed. It was the mind control potion!

Chapter 6

Danny stared as Loz's eyes turned glassy. "What do you command?" she asked.

"No! Loz!" Danny cried helplessly. He had to do something to stop Marissa and get everyone back to normal—but what? Loz was the clever one!

"Your turn," Marissa smiled, walking towards Danny with the bottle of green mind control potion.

"No!" Danny yelled desperately. "Dad! PLEASE! Let me go!" Suddenly he had an idea!

Danny tickled him!

Dad squirmed, then he giggled, then he shook with laughter, loosening his grip. "Ha! Ha ha!"

Danny quickly wriggled from his grasp and ran to the door—but it was locked!

Marissa chuckled. "There's no way out."

Danny looked around desperately, but there were no windows, no other doors, and everyone was crowding in on him with their glassy expressions. He was cornered! Marissa was right. There was no way out!

"Now be a good boy," Marissa smiled, holding out the bottle. "And take your medicine."

Danny looked around once more, then sighed heavily. "Okay. It seems I have no choice."

"Good boy," Marissa grinned as he took the bottle. "Maybe you're not as foolish as I thought."

Danny unscrewed the bottle, took a deep breath... then lunged at Marissa!

Startled, Marissa backed away, tumbling to the floor as Danny jumped on her, trying to pour the green liquid into her mouth.

"Stop!" Marissa yelled. "Stop him! Grab him!"

But to Danny's surprise, no one moved. They all just stood still, watching. Marissa's hands flew to her hair and she gasped. "My headband!"

Danny spotted her silver headband on the floor a few feet away. It must have fallen off when he knocked her over!

"So *that's* how you're controlling them!" Danny cried, grinning. He grabbed the headband, and put it on his own head.

"No!" Marissa screeched, struggling to her feet and reaching for Danny.

"Dad, grab her!" Danny ordered, and to his delight, Dad obeyed!

"Let go of me, you fool!" Marissa yelled, squirming, but Dad was too strong.

Danny grinned.

"Prime Minister, unlock the door and call the police." Danny said. "Tell them to release Mum and come here to arrest Marissa."

The Prime Minister nodded and pulled out his phone.

"What do you command?" Loz asked, glassy-eyed.

Danny shrugged, then a mischievous grin spread across his face.

Chapter 7

"Danny, you are the most amazing brother in the whole world!" Loz gushed. "You're so much smarter than I am!"

"Aw, shucks!" Danny grinned. "Now your turn, PM! And maybe add a toffee reward?"

"You are the cleverest boy I have ever met," the Prime Minister said. "I would like to reward you with a lifetime supply of toffees!"

"Oh, well, if you insist!" Danny beamed.

"Danny! What on earth is going on?" Mum asked, bursting into the room with the police, just as the Prime Minister and Loz were both bowing to him.

"Oh, um... nothing!" Danny said, taking off the silver headband quickly and snapping it in two.

Immediately, Loz, Dad, the Prime Minister and security guard blinked and looked around in a daze.

"What happened?" Dad asked, releasing Marissa.

"How did I get here?" the Prime Minister frowned.

"This woman was controlling your minds," Danny said, pointing at Marissa as she ran for the exit. "Stop her!"

"Nonsense! He's making it up!" Marissa protested, as a policewoman blocked the door.

"He's not! We have proof." Loz showed the police the video on her phone.

The Prime Minister gasped.

"You're under arrest!" the policewoman frowned, handcuffing Marissa.

"I'm so glad you're all okay!" Mum beamed, hugging Danny, Loz and Dad.

"And I'm glad you're not in trouble anymore, Mum," Loz said. "All thanks to Danny!"

"Well done, lad," the Prime Minister said, patting Danny's shoulder. "Not only did you rescue us—you saved the whole country!"

Danny beamed.

★★★

Dad and the Prime Minister shaved off their weird beards, just in case; Marissa was taken to jail; and, once everything was back to normal, the judges made their final decisions.

The Prime Minister stepped on to the stage to present the trophy.

"It's been a very eventful day!" he said. "It was a very difficult competition to judge. There were so many wonderful inventions, so in the end we have decided to award more than one prize."

Loz held her breath and Danny crossed his fingers tightly as they looked at Mum.

"The winners are... the DNA tracker!"

Loz clapped and Danny whooped as the scientist hurried onto the stage, smiling. After all, without the tracker they'd never have found Marissa and stopped her evil plans!

"And..." the Prime Minister continued, his eyes twinkling as he paused for effect. "The beard serum!"

"Go Mum!" Danny cheered and Loz clapped as Mum hesitantly climbed onto the stage.

"Thank you so much!" she beamed. She looked so happy!

"And there's one final, very special award," the Prime Minister continued. "For extreme bravery and inventiveness at a very young age—Danny and Loz!"

"What?!" Loz gasped, blushing, as Danny grabbed her hand and bounded onto the stage.

"Do we get a reward too?" Danny asked.

"Yes, you should," the Prime Minister smiled. "Hmm... what would you like?"

"Well..." Danny began.

"I know..." the Prime Minister said, a strange smile on his face. "How about a lifetime supply of toffees?"

Danny burst out laughing. "That would be perfect! How did you ever guess?!"

Discussion Points

1. What is Mum's beard serum meant to do?

2. How is Marissa able to control everyone after they have the mind control potion?

    a) With a hairband

    b) With a special watch

    c) With an electronic device

3. What was your favourite part of the story?

4. Who eats the never-ending toffee?

5. Why do you think Marissa used Mum's beard serum for her own potion?

6. Who was your favourite character and why?

7. There were moments in the story when **things weren't what they seemed.** Where do you think the story shows this most?

8. What do you think happens after the end of the story?

Book Bands for Guided Reading

The Institute of Education book banding system is a scale of colours that reflects the various levels of reading difficulty. The bands are assigned by taking into account the content, the language style, the layout and phonics. Word, phrase and sentence level work is also taken into consideration.

The Maverick Readers Scheme is a bright, attractive range of books covering the pink to grey bands. All of these books have been book banded for guided reading to the industry standard and edited by a leading educational consultant.

To view the whole Maverick Readers scheme, visit our website at

www.maverickearlyreaders.com

Or scan the QR code to view our scheme instantly!

Maverick Chapter Readers

(From Lime to Grey Band)